AESOP'S FABLES

The Ant and
the Grasshopper

Adapted by Ronne Randall
Illustrated by Louise Gardner

p

Grasshopper was a lively, happy insect, who didn't have a care in the world. He spent the long summer days relaxing in the sunshine or bouncing and dancing through the grass.

"Come and play!"
he said to Bee one day.

"I'd love to," said Bee, "but I'm *much* too busy. If I don't gather this pollen, we bees won't be able to make honey. Then, when winter comes, we'll have nothing to eat."

"Well, work if you want to," said Grasshopper. "But *I'd* rather play!"

And off he hopped.

Then, Grasshopper saw Ladybug
crawling along a leaf.

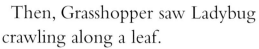

"Come and play!"

he called.

"Sorry, Grasshopper, not
today," replied Ladybug.
"I'm looking after the roses.
They depend on us to guard
them from greenfly!"

"Well, I think you're silly to spend this beautiful day working!" said Grasshopper, hopping away.

Grasshopper went happily on his way, until he saw Ant, who was struggling to carry some grain on her back.

"Why are you working so hard?" asked Grasshopper. "It's such a sunny day! **Come and play!**"

"I have no time, Grasshopper," said Ant. "I have to take this grain back to my nest, so that my family and I have enough food when winter comes. Have you built your nest yet?"

"Nest?" laughed Grasshopper. "Who needs a nest when life in the great outdoors is *so* wonderful? And there's plenty of food – why should I worry?" And off he hopped.

At night, while the other insects slept, Grasshopper sang and danced under the moonlight.

"Come and play!" he called to Spider, who was the only one awake.

"Sorry, Grasshopper," said Spider.
"I have a web to spin. Can't stop now!"

"Suit yourself!" said Grasshopper,
as he danced away.

Day after day, Grasshopper played, while the other insects worked.

And, night after night, he danced and sang while the others tried to sleep. The other insects were fed up.

"Stop that noise!"

shouted Bee, one night. "You're keeping the whole hive awake!"

"Yes, be quiet!"

said Ladybug.

"And *I'm* trying to get my babies to sleep!" cried Ant.

As the summer went on, the long, sunny days began to get shorter and cooler. But lazy Grasshopper hardly noticed. He was still *too* busy enjoying himself.

One day, Grasshopper saw Ant with her seven little children. They were all carrying food back to their nest.

"My, look at all your helpers," said Grasshopper.

"Well, we're running out of time," puffed Ant. "What are you doing about building a nest and storing food for the winter?"

"Oh, I can't be bothered," said Grasshopper. "There's lots of food around now, so why worry?"

The days passed quickly and it wasn't long before Grasshopper saw Bee again, buzzing busily around the flowers. Her feet were covered in yellow pollen.

"You're in a hurry," said Grasshopper.

"I certainly am," buzzed Bee. "I have to bring more pollen back to the hive while I can still get it. Summer won't last forever, you know!"

"I don't know what everyone's so worried about!" said Grasshopper. And off he went, leaving Bee to buzz back to her hive.

That night, there was a chill in the air and Grasshopper didn't feel like dancing.

"Maybe you'd better start getting ready for winter," warned Spider.

It was getting colder, but Grasshopper didn't want to think about that now.

"There's still *loads* of time for that!"
said Grasshopper and he began to sing.

Soon the trees began to lose their leaves. Grasshopper was spending more time looking for food and less time having fun, but there wasn't much food to be found.

One afternoon, Ant and her children scurried across his path, each carrying a fat, ripe seed.

"Where did you find those?" asked Grasshopper, eagerly. "Are there any more?"

"There are plenty over there," said Ant, pointing. "When are you going to make a nest? Winter will be here soon!"

"I'm too hungry to think about that now," said Grasshopper, rushing towards the seeds and gobbling down as many as he could.

A few days later, it began to snow.

Ladybug was in her nest, fast asleep.

Bee was in her hive, sipping sweet honey with her friends and relations.

Grasshopper was cold and all alone.
He was hungry and there wasn't a crumb
of food to be found anywhere!

Spider looked down from his web.
"What are you going to do now?" he asked.

It began to snow harder. "I know," said Grasshopper. "Ant will help me. She has plenty of food."

So he set out to look for Ant's nest.

Once a blackbird swooped down and almost caught him, but Grasshopper just managed to duck out of its way. Now he was cold, hungry and frightened, too.

At last, Grasshopper found Ant's cosy nest, safe and warm beneath a rock.

Ant came out to see him. "What do you want?" she asked.

"Please, Ant," said Grasshopper, "have you any food to spare?"

Ant looked at him. "All summer long, while my family and I worked hard to gather food and prepare our nest, what did you do?"

"I played and had fun, of course," said Grasshopper. "That's what summer is for!"

"Well, you were wrong, weren't you," said Ant. "If you play all summer, then you must go hungry all winter."

"Yes," said Grasshopper, sadly, as a tiny tear fell from the corner of his eye. "I have learned my lesson now. I just hope it isn't too late!"

Ant's heart softened. "Okay, come on in," she said. "And I'll find some food for you."

Grasshopper gratefully crawled into the warm nest, where Ant and her family shared their food with him.

By the time Spring came around, Grasshopper was fat and fit and ready to start building a nest of his very own!